The Music Box Mystery

THE BOBBSEY TWINS®

THE
MUSIC BOX
MYSTERY

Laura Lee Hope

Illustrated by John Speirs

WANDERER BOOKS
Published by
Simon & Schuster, Inc., New York

Manufactured in the United States of America
10 9 8 7 6 5 4 3 2

WANDERER and colophon are registered trademarks
of Simon & Schuster, Inc.

THE BOBBSEY TWINS is a trademark of Stratemeyer Syndicate,
registered in the United States Patent and Trademark Office

Library of Congress Cataloging in Publication Data

Hope, Laura Lee.
The music box mystery.

(The Bobbsey twins; 9)
Summary: When Flossie receives a music box that
may have been intended as a gift for someone else,
the twins quickly realize that a mystery is involved.
[1. Mystery and detective stories. 2. Twins—
Fiction] I. Title. II. Series: Hope, Laura Lee.
Bobbsey twins (1980–   ) ; 9.
PZ7.H772Mu 1983   [Fic]   83-10329
ISBN 0-671-43589-2 (pbk.)

Contents

1. Surprise Package 7
2. Missing Girl 18
3. Seal Squabble 30
4. The Sea Sprite 41
5. Rain on the Roof 54
6. An Exciting Discovery 64
7. The Stowaway 74
8. Down the Mousehole 88
9. The Twirly Clue 96
10. Secret Treasure 110

Surprise Package

"Here comes the mailman!" cried six-year-old Freddie Bobbsey, looking out the window.

His blonde twin, Flossie, ran to open the front door. "Anything for me?" she asked.

The mailman handed her some letters and said, "Indeed there is, honey!" Reaching into his bag, he pulled out a brown-paper-wrapped package.

"Ooh!" squealed the little girl. "What's this?"

The mailman chuckled. "I guess you

might call it a surprise package. That means there's only one way to find out!"

Flossie ran to show the package to her mother.

"Hey, is that for you?" said Freddie.

"I guess so. Is it, Mother?"

A puzzled smile came over Mrs. Bobbsey's face as she read the writing on the package. "My goodness, how odd. There's no name on it."

"Then who's it for?" Freddie persisted.

"It just says 'The little girl who lives at this address,'" his mother replied. "So I suppose that means Flossie."

"Are you sure it doesn't say 'The *big* girl'?" called out a laughing voice. The dark-haired twelve-year-old twins, Nan and Bert, had just come into the room. Nan's eyes were twinkling as she spoke.

"No, I do believe it's for Flossie," said Mrs. Bobbsey, smiling back at Nan and her brother.

"How come?" Bert asked. "Today

isn't Flossie's birthday."

"I'm afraid we'll just have to wait till she opens it, dear, to answer that question."

Flossie was eagerly pulling off the brown paper wrapping. Inside was a cardboard box.

"C'mon, open that, too!" Freddie urged, jumping up and down and clapping his hands.

Flossie did and took out another box. This one was made of wood. Its hinged cover was decorated with fancy carving and inlaid with shiny mother-of-pearl.

"Ooh, isn't it be-yoo-tiful!" she gasped.

The box had four small legs, one at each corner.

"What's in it?" said Flossie's older brother. Everyone else was just as interested as Bert.

Flossie held her breath and lifted the cover. A lovely, tinkling melody began to play!

"There's music in it, that's what!" she blurted in delight.

All the children and Mrs. Bobbsey listened as the music box played on. The tinkly notes reminded Nan of a graceful fountain splashing in an old-fashioned garden.

"What a lovely piece!" she murmured softly.

Flossie's face fell as the music ended. "Is that all?"

"You should have closed the box up quick before all the music got out!" Freddie scolded.

"Don't be silly!" Bert chuckled. "You just have to wind it up some more, Flossie."

He turned the box over. Sure enough, there was a winding key on the bottom. Flossie wound it up one or two turns. When she set the box down and opened the cover, the music began to play again as beautifully as ever.

"Oh, goody!" the little girl exclaimed,

her face wreathed in smiles. "Can I keep putting more music in just by winding it up?"

Bert grinned and ruffled her golden curls. "As often as you like, honey. Just don't wind it up too tight."

"I wonder who sent Flossie the music box?" said Nan.

"So do I," said her mother. "It's certainly puzzling."

Nan had picked up the brown wrapping and was eyeing it curiously. "The address label says it came from Pym's Antique Shop on Main Street."

"Didn't that just go out of business?" put in Bert.

"Yes, the shop closed last month when old Mr. Pym died," Mrs. Bobbsey replied. "That's what I don't understand. A story in the newspaper said his will left everything to the Lakeport Junior League, to be sold for charity."

"Golly, that's right!" Nan snapped her fingers. "And the auction's today—I remember now. Some of the girls were talking about it. Jane Shelby said her sister was hoping to pick up some things quite cheaply there, to sell at her weekend flea market stand."

Nan looked thoughtful and added, "Maybe if Bert and I went to the auction, we could find out who sent Flossie the music box."

"Take us, too!" Flossie and Freddie begged.

Nan glanced at Mrs. Bobbsey. "Okay if we do, Mom?"

"Of course, dear. But you two little ones hang on to Nan's and Bert's hands when you're crossing the street."

"We will!" the small twins promised.

The antique shop looked busy that morning. People were going in and out. Some came out with objects they had bought at the sale.

The twins saw a man lug a rocking chair out of the store and load it into his pickup truck. Soon afterwards, a lady came out carrying a small table which she carefully put into the back of her station wagon.

Freddie tugged Bert's arm. "Hey, we'd better hurry up, or everything will be gone!"

"Don't worry," said Bert. "We aren't planning to buy anything."

Through the shop window the twins could see a man standing at a table in the front of the store. People were gathered around, watching as the Junior League ladies brought out the things to be sold, one by one, for the customers to inspect. The man had a small wooden hammer. He would point to each object and ask how much anyone was willing to pay for it.

"He's the auctioneer," Nan told Flossie and Freddie. As the Bobbsey twins went inside, they could hear the customers calling out how much money they were willing to pay.

When no one would offer any more money, the auctioneer would point to the highest bidder, pound his little hammer on the table, and shout "Sold!"

The dusty shop was crammed with old furniture, mirrors, paintings, china, kerosene lamps, brass candlesticks and the kind of knickknacks people show off in glass cabinets in their homes. The little twins' eyes bugged as they gazed at all the different items.

"Oh, look at those old dollies!" cooed Flossie.

Freddie was staring at a tall Japanese vase. It was decorated with painted birds and animals and ladies in kimonos and fierce-looking Japanese warriors.

"Guess how much that vase costs," said Bert.

Freddie shrugged. "I give up."

"One hundred dollars."

"Wow!"

Many items, like the vase, had price tags in case customers did not want to wait and bid for them at auction. Junior League ladies were moving around the shop, waiting on these customers.

"There's Mrs. Dalton," said Nan. "Maybe she can help us."

The pleasant-faced young woman knew all about the music box. "We found it on a shelf in the back of the store," she explained. "There was a card on it saying: 'To be saved for this little girl,' with her name and address on a piece of paper taped to the card. But when we pulled off the tape, the name was too smudged to read. So all we could do was send the music box to 'The little girl who lives at this address.'"

"It was a wonderful surprise for Flossie," said Nan, "but we never knew old Mr. Pym."

Mrs. Dalton sighed. "That card must have been written years ago. I suppose now we'll never find out who he meant."

Bert spoke up. "I remember Dad saying once that he bought our house from the Wardells. Maybe the little girl was someone in their family. I'll ask him to-night."

"If he doesn't know, don't worry about it," said Mrs. Dalton. "Mr. Pym's will was read weeks ago. Since the Wardells haven't called for the music box yet, I doubt they ever will."

"Thanks for sending it to me," said Flossie.

"You're welcome, dear." The Junior League lady gave her a hug. "I can't imagine any nicer little girl that Mr. Pym could have—"

Her words were interrupted by a warning cry from Bert. "Look out, Freddie!"

The little boy had lost his balance. He was tumbling straight toward the Japanese vase!

2

Missing Girl

Flossie moaned and put her hands over her eyes. She could not bear to see the beautiful vase get knocked over and broken! Why did Freddie always get into such awful scrapes?

But Freddie didn't knock over the vase. Just in time, a man's hand reached out and grabbed the little boy to save him from falling!

"Oh, my goodness," gasped Mrs. Dalton. "What a close call! Thank you for catching him, Mr. Smith!"

Bert thanked the man, too, and added

sharply, "You should be more careful, Freddie!"

"I *was* careful," said his little brother, "but someone pushed me—real hard!" Freddie looked as if he might burst into angry tears.

"The little fellow's right," said Mr. Smith. "I saw a big boy give him a nasty shove. That's why I grabbed him."

As the Bobbseys looked around, they saw the boy who had pushed Freddie elbowing his way toward the door.

"It's Danny Rugg!" cried Nan.

"What a dirty trick!" Bert fumed.

Danny, who was in the same grade as the older twins, liked to pick on smaller children. He was known as the school bully. More than once, Bert had had to teach him a lesson.

As he reached the doorway, Danny turned and made a face at the Bobbseys. Then he ran off, laughing like a loon.

Bert doubled up his fists. "I ought to punch that pest right in the nose!" He would have gone after the bully, but Nan stopped him.

"Don't, Bert," she pleaded. "You can't catch him now."

Bert knew his sister was right, so he cooled off. With so many people in the way, by the time he squirmed past them to the door Danny would probably be out of sight.

"Don't worry," soothed Mrs. Dalton. "I'll see that that boy isn't allowed back in the store."

The man who had caught Freddie held out his hand to the Bobbseys. "My name's Don Smith," he said. "I'm a reporter for the *Lakeport News*."

He was a curly-haired young man with a friendly grin. A camera was hanging on a strap around his neck. Bert and Nan shook hands with him and thanked him again. So did the younger twins.

"Do you write all the news in the paper?" asked Flossie.

"Well, not all of it, honey." Don Smith laughed. "But I do write some of the stories that people read there. In fact I'd like to write one about you and the music box."

He explained that he had overheard the conversation between the Bobbseys and Mrs. Dalton. "This antique store of Mr. Pym's has been here a long time, hasn't it?" he turned to ask the Junior League lady.

"Oh my, yes," she replied. "At least as long as I've lived in Lakeport."

"So here's a music box that was meant as a present for some other little girl long ago," said Mr. Smith. "But even though she may live far away now and has forgotten all about the music box, it didn't get sold off with everything else in the shop. This morning it became a happy surprise present for another little girl named Flossie Bobbsey!"

He aimed his camera at Flossie and

went on, "I was sent here to write about the auction, but I think this will make an even better story!"

"Gee whiskers!" said Freddie. "Will my sister's picture be in the paper?"

"Let's hope so." Don Smith grinned. "She's certainly cute enough to have her picture in the paper, don't you think?"

"How do I know?" said Freddie. "She looks okay, I guess."

Don Smith snapped a picture of Flossie and the music box, and a closeup picture of just the music box, and also one of Flossie and Freddie holding it between them. Then he took a picture of all the twins and Mrs. Dalton.

"What if we find out the music box was meant for someone in the Wardell family," Bert asked, "and she comes back to Lakeport to get it?"

Don Smith chuckled and clapped him on the back. "Then we'll have another great story!"

Mr. Bobbsey ran a lumberyard in Lakeport, and when he came home from work that day, he was surprised to see his little daughter's picture in the evening paper. "So now my little girl is famous!" he declared.

Flossie squealed with delight as he tossed her high in the air and caught her in a bear hug.

"Me next, me next!" cried Freddie, jumping up and down.

At the dinner table, Bert asked his father about the family that had lived in the house before the Bobbseys moved in. "Didn't you say their name was Wardell, Dad?"

"That's right." Mr. Bobbsey nodded as he helped himself to more roast beef and mashed potatoes. "Mr. and Mrs. Wardell were elderly people. They sold the house because Mr. Wardell had retired from his job, and they wanted to move to Florida."

"Did they have a little girl?" Nan asked.

"Yes, a little granddaughter. You know, I'd forgotten all about her. It was rather a sad story." Mr. Bobbsey said that the child had run away on the very day he came to sign the purchase papers for the house.

"Naturally the Wardells were very upset," he recalled. "They had already bought their plane tickets and were to fly to Florida the next morning."

"Did their little granddaughter turn up before they left?"

"I never found out." Mr. Bobbsey sighed regretfully. "Your mother and I were busy moving, and the Wardells were gone by the time we arrived. Of course, all this happened before you and Bert were born, Nan, so that little girl would be quite a young lady by now."

The doorbell rang while the Bobbseys were still at the table. Dinah Johnson, who helped Mrs. Bobbsey with the cooking and housekeeping, went to answer the door.

"A gentleman wants to see little Miss Flossie," she reported, looking slightly puzzled. "It's something to do with that music box."

The caller turned out to be a man with a bushy mustache. He said his name was Mr. Crane.

"You came to see our little girl?" Mrs. Bobbsey inquired.

"I came for the music box, that's all."

"I'm afraid I don't understand."

"Well, you see, I've had my eye on that music box for a long time," Mr. Crane replied. "Old Mr. Pym finally promised to sell it to me for twenty dollars."

"But the lady at the auction told my children there was a note attached to the music box saying it was to be saved for some little girl."

"Sure, sure, I know all that. But Mr. Pym was planning to close his shop and

go out of business soon, anyhow, even if he hadn't died, and he promised me if she didn't show up to claim the box by that time, I could have it."

Mr. Crane said that he had paid Pym ten dollars toward the purchase price of twenty dollars. "And I'll pay your little girl the other ten when she gives me the box," he added.

The mustached caller seemed tense and fidgety. He had a little pocketknife on a chain with a tiny flashlight attached to the other end, and he kept twirling them as he spoke.

Mr. Bobbsey had listened quietly so far, but now he said, "I suppose you have some proof of your story?"

"Proof?" Mr. Crane looked uncomfortable. "What do you mean?"

"Didn't Mr. Pym give you a receipt for the ten dollars you paid him?"

"No, why should he?" said the mustached man, twirling his chain. "We were old friends."

"But we've never seen you before,"

Mr. Bobbsey pointed out.

"Look, I'll give your kid the whole twenty dollars! That's fair enough, isn't it?"

Mr. Bobbsey smiled politely. "We'll think it over. In the meantime, maybe you can think of some way to prove your story."

Mr. Crane glared at the twins' father. Then he stuffed his knife and flashlight back in his pocket and stalked out of the house. The front door slammed angrily behind him.

"I didn't like that man," said Flossie.

"Neither did I," said Mr. Bobbsey, with a twinkle in his eye. "So that makes two of us."

"I'd say that makes *all* of us," Mrs. Bobbsey corrected. The whole family burst out laughing.

The Bobbseys were watching television a little while later when the doorbell rang again. This time their visitor was the *Lakeport News* reporter, Don Smith.

"How did you like your picture, honey?" he asked Flossie.

"Super! Daddy liked it, too."

"How come all our pictures didn't get in?" complained Freddie.

"Editors are stingy with space," the newsman explained. "Mine thought the story was great, but he still wouldn't give me room for any more pictures."

Bert repeated what Mr. Bobbsey had told the twins about the Wardells.

"Hmm, that's interesting," said Don Smith. "It may tie in with another story I'm working on. In fact that's why I'm here."

"To find out about the Wardells?" asked Nan.

Don Smith nodded. "Yes. You see, I cover town hall, so I've been digging into our back files for feature stories about the town council—and recently I came across a mystery that concerns someone named Wardell."

3

Seal Squabble

Flossie clapped her hands and exclaimed, "Oh, goody! We *love* mysteries!"

Don Smith grinned. "And from all I hear, you Bobbseys are pretty good at solving them, too. Anyhow, this one started out with a squabble over the town seal."

"The town seal?" Freddie cocked his head in surprise. "I didn't know towns had seals. Where do they keep them? In the park?"

His question brought a ripple of laughter from the grownups and the two older twins.

"Mr. Smith doesn't mean the kind of seal that has flippers and swims in the water," explained Bert.

"What other kind is there?"

"Freddie, you've seen Mother seal her letters with a blob of pretty colored wax, haven't you?" put in Nan.

"Sure." The little blond boy nodded. "Then she stamps the wax with a picture of a butterfly."

"That's right. Well, the thing she stamps the picture with is called a seal. And that's what Mr. Smith meant . . . except, I guess, a town seal would be bigger and more important-looking."

"Yes, and it wouldn't be used to seal letters. It would be used to stamp official papers," Mr. Bobbsey explained. "And the seal picture might also appear on the side of the town's police cars. But not in Lakeport, because we don't have a town seal."

"About fifteen years ago, though," said Don Smith, "a wealthy man named Ashton offered Lakeport a seal of its own —and it was quite good-looking, too. He'd paid an artist to design it. But a lot of people didn't like the design."

"Why not?" said Bert.

"Well, you see, it included the Ashton family's crest, or coat of arms. Ashton felt that was perfectly okay, because back in Indian days, when this part of the country was pretty much a wilderness, the first settlers who came here were members of the Ashton family."

Just then, the Bobbseys' little fox terrier, Waggo, came bounding into the living room. He went straight to Don Smith and began sniffing his pant legs and shoes.

"Hi there, boy," said the reporter.

Flossie beamed. "He's 'vestigating you."

As Waggo's tail began to wag, Freddie said, "He likes you."

"Yes, dear. But you two sit down again and listen. It isn't polite to interrupt," Mrs. Bobbsey said gently.

The two young twins took Waggo and went back to join Nan and Bert on the big flowered sofa.

Don Smith grinned. "Well, anyhow, some people weren't too thrilled with the town seal that Mr. Ashton offered Lakeport. They thought Ashton was too puffed up with his own importance, and considered himself a bigshot. They said the seal made it look as though his family *owned* Lakeport."

"What did Mr. Ashton do?" Bert inquired.

"Oh, he knew it wouldn't be easy getting the town council on his side. So he tried to sweeten his offer. He said if they would accept his design as the town's official seal, he would present Lakeport with an unusual treasure."

"Wow!" Freddie's eyes grew big. "What kind of treasure?"

"That's part of the mystery," said Don Smith. "Nobody knows to this day what he was talking about. The trouble was, you see, that Ashton did put on airs and act like a bigshot. He was such a loud, blustery, boastful sort of guy that folks didn't like him. He made so many people mad that the town council took a vote and turned down his offer."

"Poor Mr. Ashton," murmured Nan, who was too sweet a girl to dislike anyone very much. "I'll bet that made *him* awfully mad."

"It sure did. He was furious. He told the *Lakeport News* that his seal had been rejected just because people were jealous of the Ashtons. He said if the public or the news reporters ever got to the root of the matter, they would see just what fools the town councilors were. Then he sold all his property here in Lakeport and moved to California."

"Is that where he's living now?" Bert inquired.

"I guess so. Nobody knows. Neither he nor the treasure he offered Lakeport has been heard of since. In fact, as I say, no one even knows what kind of treasure he was talking about."

"But you said the mystery concerned someone named Wardell," Nan reminded the reporter.

"That's right." Don Smith nodded. "And that's why I came to see you Bobbseys. I've gone over the town council records very carefully. At the council meeting when Ashton's seal was turned down, he said he'd had the design for his seal drawn by an artist named Belinda Wardell."

"Belinda Wardell?" echoed Bert, glancing first at his sister and then at their father. "Golly, maybe she's related to the Wardells who lived here before Dad bought this house."

"Exactly," said Don Smith. "If we could find her, maybe she could provide a clue to the unknown treasure. At any rate, she's the only lead I have to work on. Unfortunately there are no Wardells listed in the Lakeport telephone directory or the town records. That's why I was interested, Bert, when you mentioned the Wardells at the antique shop this morning."

"How about it, Dad?" said Bert. "Does that name, Belinda Wardell, ring any bells in your memory?"

Mr. Bobbsey shook his head thoughtfully. "I'm afraid not, Son."

Neither he nor his wife could recall any Belinda Wardell. Nor could they remember ever hearing of an artist by that name, in or out of Lakeport.

At that moment, Dinah came into the cozy living room carrying a tray with coffee and cream and sugar and big glasses of milk for the twins. And there was a big plate of her freshly made chocolate walnut cookies.

Mr. Bobbsey was a member of the town council, and while everyone was sipping and nibbling he remarked, "You know, Don, I do remember hearing old-timers at the town hall talk about that dispute over Ashton's seal."

"Yes, a few people still remember him," said the reporter. "I guess he was quite a character."

Mr. Bobbsey chuckled. "Matter of fact, the town clerk says Ashton wasn't really such a bad fellow. He had quite a sense of humor and even cracked a few jokes at the council meeting. The trouble was, he rubbed people the wrong way."

Freddie and Flossie had been feeding Waggo bits of their cookies. Now they could see that he wanted some exercise. So they asked to be excused and took him out in the backyard.

While they watched the little dog run around smelling everything, Flossie said, "I wonder what rubbing people the wrong way means?"

Freddie frowned. "Maybe it's like our kitten. She doesn't like us to pet her backwards and mess up her fur."

By the time the curly-haired blond twins had talked this over, while sitting in the wooden garden swing, and played a game of catch the ball with Waggo, it was time to go in.

They discovered that Mr. Smith had gone. Mr. and Mrs. Bobbsey were still chatting in the living room with Bert and Nan.

"By the way," said Mr. Bobbsey, "did you know there's a picture of Mr. Ashton outside the town hall?"

"Whereabouts?" asked Bert.

Mr. Bobbsey was about to tell, but then with a smile he changed his mind. "Let's just say there's another little mystery for you detectives to solve. See if you can find it."

That night, in the pink and white bedroom she shared with Flossie, Nan turned out the lamp on the nightstand between their beds and then switched on her small radio.

"Better keep it low, or Mom and Dad will hear it," Flossie whispered. She herself wasn't listening. She was eager to solve the mystery Mr. Bobbsey had given the twins, and was deciding where she and Freddie should look for Mr. Ashton's picture tomorrow. Her head began to nod.

Suddenly Nan said, "Listen, Flossie!"

The little girl quickly sat up in bed in surprise. The radio was playing the same lovely tune they had heard the music box play that morning!

4

The Sea Sprite

"That's what my music box plays!" Flossie exclaimed in delight.

"Shh!" Nan warned with a finger to her lips.

The girls listened in happy silence, enjoying the charming melody. Even when played by an orchestra, with violins instead of music box notes, the piece had a gay, tinkly sound. "It's sort of like a minuet," Nan murmured dreamily.

"What's a minny-wet?" Flossie whispered.

Nan giggled. "An old-fashioned dance

that ladies and gentlemen danced long ago."

"What's the song's name?"

"I don't know, I didn't hear. Maybe the announcer will repeat it when the music's over."

The two sisters waited and listened. But Nan's hope was dashed when the announcer's voice came on again, saying, "And now, in response to many requests from our listeners, here is 'A Little Night Music,' by Mozart. . . ."

"I guess we're out of luck, Flossie dear," Nan whispered.

There was no reply. Nan smiled as a faint snoring sound came from her little sister's bed.

Nan herself had no memory of drifting off to sleep. But suddenly she was awakened by the thud of heavy steps dashing downstairs.

Golly, what's going on? she wondered.

Getting up, Nan scampered across the

floor and opened her bedroom door to look out. Other doors were opening, too. Mr. Bobbsey and the boy twins had also been awakened by the noise.

"What's wrong, Daddy?" Nan asked.

"I don't know. That must have been Sam running downstairs. You children stay here while I go and see." Dinah Johnson and her husband Sam, who worked for Mr. Bobbsey at the lumberyard, lived on the top floor of the Bobbseys' house.

Bert and Freddie, impatient to find out what was going on, sneaked down far enough to peek around the corner of the staircase landing.

Presently Bert passed the word to his sister that it was okay to go on downstairs. Nan flung on her bathrobe. Flossie, who was also awake by now, went along with her big sister.

"Sam heard someone trying to break into the house," their father reported.

The elderly Mr. Johnson, who had pulled on trousers and a jacket, was just coming back in.

"Any sign of him?" Mr. Bobbsey asked.

"No, sir. Whoever it was, I reckon he ran off with his tail between his legs when he heard folks waking up. But he left something behind."

Sam Johnson related that he had heard a noise below his window. "I looked out and saw someone trying to pry open a basement window."

"Did you get a look at him?" Bert asked.

"Nope, it was too dark. But he must have been disguised, anyhow."

"Disguised?" Nan echoed in surprise. "How do you know that, Sam?"

"Because I found this in the flower bed." Sam held up what looked like a clump of hair.

"It's a fake mustache!" Bert exclaimed.

"Wow! A bushy one," said Freddie, "just like that guy Mr. Crane had!"

Mr. Bobbsey examined the mustache, which had a sticky patch to hold it in place. "You're right, son," he said. "I'd call this clear evidence that Crane lied to us about the music box."

Mrs. Bobbsey and Dinah had also come downstairs by this time. Dinah made cocoa to help the children get back to sleep, and gradually the household once again settled down to rest.

Next morning Flossie was outdoors wheeling her doll buggy and Freddie was playing fireman with his red fire truck, when a car drove up. A tall man with horn-rimmed glasses got out. "Hi," he said. "Is this where the Bobbseys live?"

"Yes, sir," said Flossie.

"Is your daddy home?"

"No, but Mom is," Freddie told the man.

"Good! Maybe she can help me."

Soon he was seated in the living room, talking to Mrs. Bobbsey and all four of the twins. He said he was a lawyer from Cleveland named Durkee. A friend had told him about the newspaper story concerning the music box.

"So I flew to Lakeport this morning," Mr. Durkee went on. "You see, I, too, am looking for a girl named Wardell."

Mr. Durkee explained that he was the lawyer for a boat company. Years ago, a man named Scott Wardell had sent the company plans for a new kind of sailboat that he called the Sea Sprite. The company never bothered to reply.

"The plans got mislaid, I guess," said Mr. Durkee. "But later on someone ran across them, and the company started manufacturing the Sea Sprite. Those little boats have been selling like hotcakes ever since!"

"Golly," said Nan, "I'll bet Mr. Wardell will be glad to hear the news!"

The lawyer shook his head regretfully.

"I'm afraid not, my dear. We've learned that Scott Wardell was lost at sea during a yacht race about fifteen years ago. So now we're trying to find out if he left any relatives."

Mrs. Bobbsey said, "Could the Wardell girl you're looking for be related to the Wardells who lived here before us?"

"That's exactly what we're hoping, Mrs. Bobbsey. So far we've only been able to get in touch with one member of the yacht crew who sailed in that race. He told us Scott Wardell came from this part of the country. He also recalls his mentioning a little daughter named Charlotte."

Mrs. Bobbsey related that the Wardells' little granddaughter had run away just before the Bobbseys had moved into the house. "We don't even know if she was ever found. So if she was the Charlotte Wardell you're looking for, finding her after all these years may be very difficult."

The lawyer frowned. "How very unfortunate."

"Is it important to find her, Mr. Durkee?" asked Bert.

"It would certainly be important to her, my boy. You see, part of the money the boat company earns every time they sell a Sea Sprite belongs to Scott Wardell, because he designed the boat. That money is called a royalty. By now, the company has sold so many Sea Sprites that he has thousands of dollars in royalties coming to him—or to Charlotte Wardell, if she's his only living relative."

"Gosh," said Bert, "then if you could find her, she'd be rich!"

"She would indeed," said Mr. Durkee. "That's one reason I was hoping you folks could help me. Also, I gathered from that newspaper story that you Bobbsey twins are good at solving mysteries."

Bert grinned and looked at the other twins. "We've solved a few."

"And I'm sure they'll do their best to find out what happened to the Wardell girl who used to live here," put in Mrs. Bobbsey. Then she added with a doubtful smile, "Though to be honest, I can't imagine how they'll go about it."

"Maybe we'll get an idea," Nan said hopefully.

"If you do, my dear, please let me know," said Mr. Durkee. Before leaving, he gave a phone number where he could be reached by collect call.

At noon Mrs. Bobbsey made the children egg-salad sandwiches. Dinah had baked a cherry pie. As the twins were enjoying thir lunch, Freddie said, "I wonder if old Mr. Ashton had someone to cook and serve his meals."

"Probably," said Nan. "Even if he had no family, he was rich, so he could have had servants."

"Well, if he did," said her little brother, "then maybe his servants still live around here."

"Hey, good thinking, Freddie!" said Bert. "If you're right, they may know about the treasure Mr. Ashton was going to give Lakeport!"

After lunch, Bert called Don Smith. It turned out the reporter had had the same idea. "In fact I've already tracked down Ashton's butler," he said. "His name is Tweed, and he lives over in Shoreview. I'm going to see him this afternoon. Would you twins like to come?"

"You bet!"

But the trip was disappointing. Mr. Tweed was a large, balding man with a fringe of hair around his ears. He lived alone in a small apartment. His manner was gloomy, and when Don Smith asked him questions, his replies were not very helpful.

"You don't remember the artist Mr. Ashton hired to design the town seal?" said the reporter.

The butler frowned and shook his head. "Mr. Ashton must have handled all that at his office. I don't recall any artist coming to the mansion."

"What about the treasure he promised to present to the town of Lakeport?"

Tweed shrugged. "Mr. Ashton never mentioned it to me. Whatever it was, he probably took it to California when the mansion was sold."

"He was sure a big help," Bert grumbled as they drove off.

Don Smith dropped the older twins off at the Bobbseys' house, but Flossie and Freddie rode on downtown with the reporter. They wanted to meet their father, who had been attending a meeting of the town council that afternoon.

As they got out of the car, Don Smith pointed to a beautiful tree with fernlike leaves, planted on the lawn in front of the town hall. "There's something Mr. Ashton *did* present to Lakeport."

"You mean the tree?" asked Freddie.

"Yes, it's a ginkgo tree from China."

This reminded the little twins of the

picture of Mr. Ashton which their father had said was somewhere outside the town hall. "Let's look for it while we're waiting for Daddy," said Flossie.

"Okay!"

The two children scampered up the broad stone steps leading to the front doors. Then they looked all around the building. Freddie's keen eyes scanned each wall but could see no picture.

Suddenly he heard his little sister cry out excitedly, "Freddie! I've found it!"

5

Rain on the Roof

Flossie was standing on the thick green lawn next to the tree Don Smith had pointed out.

"Where?" Freddie demanded, running toward his sister. Then he saw that she was pointing at a big grayish-white rock, half hidden by the drooping branches of a forsythia bush.

As he came closer, he noticed a bronze plaque or tablet fixed on the rock. It bore the likeness of a man's head, with some lettering underneath. The two small twins hunched down for a better look.

"Can you read what it says?" Flossie asked her brother.

"Hmm . . . not very well," Freddie admitted, "but I think that says his name right there."

Just then the tall figure of Mr. Bobbsey emerged from the town hall and walked down the broad stone steps and across the lawn toward the twins.

"I see my clever little detectives have found it," he said, smiling.

"Flossie found it, Daddy," Freddie said truthfully as they ran to meet him.

"Only we can't read what it says." Flossie took her father's hand and tugged him toward the rock.

"Well, let's see. It says that Henry Ashton presented this ginkgo tree to Lakeport, and that the tree came from China."

"Wow," said Freddie, shading his eyes to look up at the branches. "It is kind of different-looking from most trees—especially the branches!"

"Yes, the leaves look like maidenhair ferns, so sometimes it's called the maidenhair tree." As he took his little boy and girl by the hand and led them to his car in the town hall parking lot, Mr. Bobbsey went on, "I've read that the Chinese cook the fruit from ginkgo trees and eat it."

On the way home, the twins paid special attention to all the different kinds of trees they saw.

When they arrived home, Freddie and Flossie hurried upstairs to wash for dinner because Dinah was almost ready to call everyone to the table. They had just finished drying their hands when Nan came bounding up the stairs. She looked excited!

"Guess what?" she said.

"You're late," Freddie joked to his tall, dark-haired sister.

"Yes, yes, I know. But maybe I have a clue to the music box mystery!"

As she washed her hands, Nan said

that one of her girlfriends had told her that the radio program which she and Flossie had heard in bed last night played only request numbers. "Do you know what that means?" Nan ended.

"Then someone must have *asked* the station to play that music box piece!" Flossie burst out eagerly.

"Right! And maybe—just *maybe*— that 'someone' could have been the Wardell girl who used to live here before we were born!"

Before anything more could be discussed, Mrs. Bobbsey called the children down to dinner. But later, when the family was seated around the table and Bert heard Nan's idea, he was not as hopeful as his sister.

"Think how many people must listen to that radio station," he pointed out.

"Okay, maybe lots and lots of people do," Nan conceded. "But out of all those people, how many know that particular piece? And how many would bother calling in to have it played? If the Wardell girl loved the music box and liked that tune, isn't it at least *possible* that she was the one who asked?"

Mr. Bobbsey chuckled quietly. "I'd say she's got you there, Bert. If there's any chance at all, surely it's worth checking out."

Right after dinner, Nan called Information to find out the telephone number of the radio station in Cleveland that she and Flossie had listened to the night before. Then she dialed the number and told the switchboard operator why she was calling.

"Would you like to speak to the disc jockey who broadcasts that show?" said the operator. "He's in the studio now."

"Yes, please, if I may," Nan replied.

A young man's voice soon came on the line. Nan said, "Last night you played a certain tune, and I'm wondering if you can tell me who requested it."

"Which tune was that?" the disc jockey asked.

"Well, I don't know the name of it, but

it goes like this." Nan hummed the melody.

"Oh, yes, that's called 'Amaryllis'," the young man said at once. But then he hesitated before answering. "May I ask why you want to know who requested it?"

Nan explained about the music box and the little girl who had run away years ago. "So now we're trying to find her, and we hope this may be a clue," she ended.

"I understand. Just hold on a minute, and I'll check through last night's program notes." After a few minutes, the young man reported that "Amaryllis" had been requested by Mr. Fred Holt of Rock Creek. "I hope he can help you," the disc jockey added before hanging up.

"What did he say?" Flossie exclaimed as she tried to read what her sister had jotted down.

"The person who requested that number wasn't anyone named Wardell," Nan said, looking disappointed. "It was a Mr.

Holt." Then she brightened. "I'm going to call him, anyhow. Maybe he's related to the Wardells."

"Oh, yes," Flossie urged.

So Nan dialed Information again and asked for the number of Fred Holt in Rock Creek. But after calling and talking to him, she hung up dejectedly.

"He doesn't know any Wardells," Nan told Flossie. "He says he requested 'Amaryllis' because he and his wife have always loved that tune."

The next morning, Flossie awoke to the patter of rain on the roof. She saw that Nan's bed was already empty, so she threw back the covers and jumped up and quickly washed and dressed herself.

"What'll we do this morning?" she asked Freddie as the two little twins ate their cereal. "It's too wet to play outside."

"I know," her brother said glumly. "Why does it have to rain when summer vacation starts?"

"If it didn't, there wouldn't be any

nice green grass or flowers," said Dinah Johnson as she served them some of her special pancakes.

"Hey, I know what!" exclaimed Freddie. "Let's play up in the attic!"

"Oh, yes, that's a wonderful idea!" agreed Flossie. "Maybe we can find some clothes to dress up in!"

So, after breakfast, she and Freddie climbed the three flights of stairs up to the attic to explore and play. Waggo tagged along with them. But after he had sniffed all around for a while, the little dog was content to lie and watch as the twins rummaged through a big old trunk.

Suddenly a shaft of sunlight fell on the open pages of a very old picture book that Flossie had just taken from the trunk. She looked up to see the sun shining through one of the attic windows.

Flossie bounded to her feet, exclaiming joyfully, "Look, Freddie! The rain has stopped!"

But after she ran to peer outside, her voice took on a different note. "Ooh, that awful Danny Rugg!"

"What's he doing now?" asked Freddie.

"He's chased Mrs. Alton's cat up a tree!"

Mrs. Alton was the Bobbseys' new neighbor. Danny was throwing stones at her calico cat, which was perched in the crook of a tree in the Bobbseys' side yard.

"Let's stop him!" Flossie cried angrily, an outraged look on her chubby little face.

She turned and ran toward the stairway. But in her haste, she tripped over a pile of old magazines and fell hard on the attic floor!

·6·

An Exciting Discovery

"Flossie, are you okay?" Freddie cried as he ran to where his sister lay sprawled on the floor. He bent down anxiously to help her.

"I'm all right," Flossie said, pushing herself up on her knees.

Just before Freddie helped her to her feet, she noticed a piece of rolled-up paper in an open space between two floorboards. Flossie wondered what it was as she dusted off her knees.

But there was no time to examine the paper now, not with Danny Rugg still teasing the cat in the tree! So Flossie and Freddie ran downstairs and outside.

"Stop throwing stones at that poor cat!" Freddie shouted at Danny.

"Yes, stop it this minute!" Flossie joined in. "You should be ashamed of yourself, you bad boy!" She shook her finger at the neighborhood bully, and Waggo barked furiously.

"Aw, shut up and go back inside before I push you both in that mud puddle over there!" sneered Danny.

He started toward the two little twins with a nasty smile as if he really intended to dunk them in the puddle. But Freddie and Flossie faced him bravely and did not run into the house.

Just then a screen door opened, and the new neighbor lady came out on her porch.

"Now just a minute! Don't touch those children!" she called to Danny. "You're twice their size, so leave them alone. What's the trouble?"

Then suddenly she saw her calico cat looking down from the crook of the tree. "Oh, my goodness, Muffin! How did you get up there?" she exclaimed and rushed down the porch steps.

"Their dog chased it up the tree," Danny lied, pointing at Waggo.

"That's not true," Freddie retorted. "You were throwing stones at Muffin."

Flossie nodded, her little chin jutting out angrily at the bully. "We were trying to stop him, Mrs. Alton," she told the neighbor lady. "That's why he got mad at us."

"Oh, you dumb Bobbseys!" Danny blurted, getting red in the face. "Just wait'll I get even with—"

But Mrs. Alton interrupted him. "Never mind that kind of talk. I'm quite sure the Bobbsey twins wouldn't let their dog hurt Muffin. Even if I didn't know them, I can see the stones there on the ground, all around the tree." She added sharply, "What's your name, young man?"

"None of your business," Danny mumbled sullenly.

"His name's Danny Rugg, and he lives over on Pine Street," Freddie spoke up.

"Well, Danny Rugg, I think you'd better go home before I call your mother," Mrs. Alton warned in a no-nonsense voice.

Danny glared and shook his fist at Freddie and Flossie. Then he stuck his hands in his pockets and slouched off down the street.

"What a naughty thing to do, throwing stones at a helpless animal," declared Mrs. Alton. With a worried frown, she turned to look up at her cat in the tree. "Thank goodness she doesn't seem to be hurt. But how am I going to get her down?"

Muffin showed no signs of wanting to come down from her perch.

"I know what!" said Flossie with a sudden hopeful smile. "We have some catnip. Our kitten likes that. I'll go and get some, and maybe Muffin will smell it and come down."

Flossie ran inside to the Bobbseys' kitchen to fetch the catnip. Meanwhile, Mrs. Alton and Freddie tried to coax the cat down. Freddie even took Waggo into the house, in case Muffin might be frightened of him. Nothing seemed to make any difference, however.

Soon Flossie returned, carrying a paper picnic plate. There was catnip on it, and Dinah had added a bit of tunafish. Muffin immediately began to look interested. After a few sniffs, she came down out of the tree and began gobbling up the tuna and catnip!

"Oh, my poor little kitty-cat," Mrs. Alton said soothingly, stroking her pet's fur. "Thank heavens you're safe."

When Muffin finished eating and started to lick her paws, Mrs. Alton picked her up and, after thanking and praising the two Bobbsey twins, carried her rescued cat into her house.

Freddie smiled at Flossie. "I'm glad Danny didn't hurt Muffin."

"Me too!" The look on Flossie's pretty little face suddenly changed. "I just remembered something, Freddie," she exclaimed. "Let's go back up to the attic. There's something up there I want to see."

Freddie went with his sister as she dashed back into the house and up the stairs. On the way, Flossie told him about the rolled-up piece of paper she had seen between the floorboards.

When they reached the attic, Freddie looked around until he found an old yardstick. Then he used it to poke the paper up out of the crack. Flossie took their find over to the window where they could see better, and unrolled the paper in the sunlight.

"It's some kind of picture!" declared Freddie.

The picture turned out to be a painting of a little girl not much older than Flossie, with long light-blonde hair in braids.

"Look," said Freddie and pointed to

the artist's initials in one corner of the painting. The letters were *B.W.*

"Oh golly! I wonder if they stand for Belinda Wardell?" said Flossie, wide-eyed.

"She's the artist who made that town seal Mr. Smith told us about!"

"I know. And maybe this little girl is Charlotte Wardell, whose daddy got the idea for that sailboat!"

The two small twins hurried downstairs with their exciting news. Bert and Nan had just returned home from the supermarket, where they had gone to shop for some things Dinah Johnson needed to make lunch. The older twins were as excited as Freddie and Flossie when they saw the picture and the artist's initials.

"I think we should tell Don Smith about this," Bert declared.

"So do I," Nan agreed. "Why don't you call him right now, Bert?"

"Good idea." Bert looked up the

number of the *Lakeport News* and phoned the reporter.

On hearing about the painting, Don Smith was keenly interested. "Sounds like you may be onto something," he said. "I have to finish writing a story and then grab a bite to eat, but I'll be over to look at it early this afternoon, okay?"

"Great. We'll look for you," Bert said and hung up.

All four Bobbsey twins were eager to hear what the reporter might have to say about the painting. About one-thirty they heard the doorbell. Nan went to answer it and led Don Smith into the living room, where her sister and brothers were waiting to show him the little girl's picture.

Just as Don Smith started to look at it, the telephone rang.

"It's for you, Nan honey," Dinah Johnson reported a few moments later.

Nan stepped out into the hallway to speak to her caller.

"This is Tom Taylor. I'm the disc jockey on that radio program you heard the other night," said a young man's voice. "You called me to find out who requested a certain number."

"Oh, yes!" said Nan. "I didn't know the name of the tune, but you told me it was 'Amaryllis'."

"That's right. You said you wanted the information because you and your family were trying to solve a mystery."

"Yes, and we still are," Nan said, "but I'm afraid we haven't solved it yet."

"Well then, here's another clue for you Bobbseys," said Tom Taylor. "I thought you might be interested to know that someone else called to ask the name of that same tune."

"Oh! Really?" Nan gasped.

"Yes . . . a young woman in Center City named Charlotte Kincaid."

The Stowaway

Charlotte! The same first name as that of the missing Wardell heiress! Nan felt a thrill of excitement. Perhaps this was the clue that the Bobbsey twins had been hoping for, the clue that would help them unravel the music box mystery!

"Thanks ever so much, Mr. Taylor!" she said. "What you've told me may be very important!"

As soon as she hung up, Nan called Information and asked for Charlotte Kincaid's telephone number. When she dialed it, a young woman answered.

"Is th-this Charlotte Kincaid?" Nan inquired a bit nervously. Her heart was beating fast.

"Yes, I'm Charlotte Kincaid. Can I help you?"

"My name is Nan Bobbsey," said the dark-haired twin, "and I'm calling from Lakeport. I'm . . . er, that is, my brothers and sister and I are trying to find someone who used to live in Lakeport. Could you tell me, please, if you know anyone named Wardell?"

"Of course! *My* name used to be Wardell, and I lived in Lakeport when I was little. But how did you guess?"

Nan explained first about the call she had received from the radio disc jockey. Then she said, "Do you mind telling me why you wanted to find out the name of that piece, 'Amaryllis'?"

"Goodness, I . . . I don't really know." For the first time, the young woman sounded rather hesitant and confused. "I guess I've always been fond of that tune.

When they played it on the radio the other night, that was the first time I'd heard it in years. So I decided to call and ask what it was. I realized this might be the only chance I'd ever have to discover its name. It certainly isn't a tune you hear very often."

"I know," Nan agreed. "I had to phone and ask. By the way, should I call you Miss Kincaid or Mrs. Kincaid?"

The young lady chuckled. "Just Miss."

Her answer puzzled Nan. If she was not married, why had she changed her name from Wardell to Kincaid? But aloud the Bobbsey girl said, "Could we come and see you, Miss Kincaid? I think we may have important news for you."

"Of course you may, Nan. You've already got me dying with curiosity!"

"Would today be okay?"

"Any time you like, dear. I'm a schoolteacher, so I'm off now for summer vacation. As far as I know, I'll be in all afternoon."

"Oh, good! Thanks ever so much." Before hanging up, Nan jotted down Miss Kincaid's address and directions for getting there. Then she ran to tell the others her exciting news.

"Wow!" said Bert. "I'll bet Mr. Durkee will be glad to hear about this. Sounds like you've found the Charlotte Wardell he's looking for."

"It certainly does," Don Smith agreed. The twins had told him about the lawyer's visit during their ride to Shoreview. "And if this was painted by Belinda Wardell," he went on, holding up the picture Flossie had found, "then this little girl may be the person you just talked to!"

"Hey, let's take that along when we go to see her," Bert suggested. "Maybe we'll be able to *see* if they're the same person."

"But that little girl in the picture will be lots older now, won't she?" put in Flossie.

"Of course," said Nan. "If this picture's been here since the Wardells left, it must have been painted at least fifteen years ago."

"Then won't she look a lot different now?"

"Sure, probably," said Bert, "but there'll still be some resemblance. Just like with you, Flossie—fifteen years from now, you may not be Daddy's little girl anymore, but you'll still look like Miss Flossie Bobbsey!"

As he spoke, Bert scooped up his little sister in his arms, twirled her around, and gave her a big bear hug. Flossie squealed with delight.

The reporter smiled as he watched the twins. "Would I be in the way if I came along?"

"Oh no, no!" said Nan, smiling back at him. "I was hoping you'd ask."

"If you'd drive us over to Center City, that would be great!" said Bert.

"Then ask your mother if it's okay,"

said Don Smith, "and let's go!"

The trip was a pleasant ride in the afternoon sunshine. Charlotte Kincaid lived in a small apartment house near the school where she taught. She turned out to be a slender, friendly young woman with lovely, long-lashed blue eyes and a warm smile. Nan thought she was beautiful.

But a surprised look came over Miss Kincaid's face when she saw a tall, curly-haired young man with the twins. He, too, looked startled.

"This is Mr. Don Smith, Miss Kincaid," said Nan. "He's a reporter for the *Lakeport News.*"

"I guess maybe I should apologize," he said, "for inviting myself along without asking your permission first."

Charlotte Kincaid smiled. "You're as welcome as your friends, the Bobbseys. Please come in, all of you, and sit down, if you can find enough chairs. I've just made a big pitcher of lemonade."

Ice cubes were bobbing in the glasses and the little twins got straws to sip through. As her guests enjoyed the refreshing drinks, Miss Kincaid talked about her childhood in Lakeport.

"I don't remember much about the house we lived in," she said. "I don't even know what street it was on. But my father worked at the local marina, where people kept their boats."

"What was his name?" Bert asked.

"Scott Wardell."

The twins looked at each other, almost bursting with excitement. There was no doubt now that they had found the heiress Mr. Durkee was searching for! But they did not interrupt her story.

"Sailing was my father's hobby," Charlotte went on. "But it brought us bad luck. He went east to Long Island to sail in a yacht race. A bad storm came up, and he was lost at sea."

"How old were you then?" Nan said in a soft voice. She and the others looked

at their pretty young hostess sympathet-
ically.

"I was about seven," Charlotte replied. "My mother was an artist and she
tried to support us, but she couldn't find
much work in Lakeport."

"Was her name Belinda Wardell, and
did she paint this?" Flossie asked, unroll-
ing the picture.

Charlotte Kincaid gasped as she saw
the painting of the little girl in pigtails.
Then her eyes filled with tears as she
nodded in reply to Flossie's question.
Everyone could see that Charlotte had
been the little girl in the picture. The
likeness was easily apparent.

She said that her mother, Belinda
Wardell, had been unable to earn
enough as an artist for them to live on. So
she had left little Charlotte with her
husband's parents while she went to
New York to seek work illustrating
books.

"Do you by any chance remember

Pym's Antique Shop in Lakeport?" put in Bert.

Miss Kincaid hesitated briefly. Then her face lit up. "Oh, yes, of course! My mother worked there sometimes. She restored old oil paintings and did other odd jobs for Mr. Pym. In fact, I think I used to go back there by myself after she went to New York . . ." Her voice trailed off into silence, and her face became thoughtful.

"Wait, please!" Nan spoke up before the conversation could resume. "Could I use your phone, Miss Kincaid?"

"Yes, help yourself, dear. It's right over there, near the closet door."

Nan dialed the Bobbseys' own number. When her mother answered, she said, "This is Nan, Mom. Will you do what I asked you now, please?"

Then she beckoned to Charlotte and held the receiver up to her ear. "Listen, please."

Charlotte's eyes widened in surprised

delight as the tinkly notes of "Amaryllis" came over the phone. She burst into a happy smile.

"Now do you remember where you first heard that tune?" Nan asked with a twinkle.

"Indeed I do, dear! On a music box like the one I'm listening to now! Don't tell me this is the one I used to hear at Mr. Pym's shop?"

Nan nodded happily. "Yes, the very same one."

"It's all coming back to me now. Oh, how well I remember it!" Charlotte said she loved to play the music box while her mother was working at the antique shop. Later, whenever she felt sad and lonesome after her mother went to New York, she would sneak back to the shop and play it over and over again. "Mr. Pym promised to save it for me until my mother could buy it."

Flossie explained how the music box had been sent to her by mistake. "But

now you can have it, Miss Kincaid," she
promised.

Charlotte hugged the pretty little girl.
"Thank you so much, dear! I would like
to see it again, just to bring back old
memories. But I want you to have it and
enjoy it just as I did."

The slender, attractive schoolteacher
told them how she used to pine for her
mother, whom she loved and missed
very much. One day a young woman
friend of Belinda's stopped by the house.
She was driving to New York and had
promised to pick up a painting palette
which Belinda had left behind.

"When no one was looking, I hid in
the back seat of her car," Charlotte went
on. "There were coats and clothes and
things back there, so it wasn't hard to
snuggle down out of sight."

"Didn't the lady discover you?" asked
Freddie with a mischievous look on his
face.

"Not until she was halfway to New

York," said Charlotte. "By then she had gone too far to turn back, so she phoned my grandparents, and went on and delivered me to my mother."

Neither Belinda Wardell nor her little daughter could bear to be parted again, so from then on Charlotte lived with her mother. Belinda eventually became a well-known artist and married again. Her second husband—a book editor named Bruce Kincaid—adopted Charlotte.

"My mother and stepfather were very happy," said Charlotte, "but they went down in a plane crash during a trip to the West Indies. When the accident happened, I was going to college in Center City. So I stayed on here as a teacher."

Don Smith had been watching her eagerly. "Do you remember your mother drawing a design for a man in Lakeport named Mr. Ashton?" he asked.

"Mr. Ashton?" Charlotte puckered her forehead. "What kind of design was it?"

"For the Lakeport town seal."

She shook her head slowly. "Not that I recall. I suppose I was too little."

The Bobbseys decided that now was the time to tell her about the fortune she would inherit from her father's boat design. Charlotte was thrilled by the news and promised to get in touch with this lawyer, Mr. Durkee, at once. But on the way home, Don Smith did not seem very happy.

"I'll bet I know what's wrong," Flossie whispered to Nan in the back seat of the car. "I think he *likes* Miss Charlotte— but if she's rich, he's afraid she won't want to marry him!"

·8·

Down the Mousehole

"I wonder how rich Miss Kincaid's going to be," Freddie blurted suddenly. It was almost as if he had overheard what his little sister was whispering about.

"What's the difference?" Nan said. "I don't think she'll let that change her." She, too, had noticed how sad and unhappy Don Smith seemed.

Bert, who was sitting in the front seat beside Don, took a look at the reporter's glum expression. "Nope, I'll bet it won't change her at all," he agreed, and then winked back at Nan, who smiled and nodded approvingly.

Don Smith heaved a sigh. "Well, I hope she does become very rich," he said, "to make up for all her unhappiness and loneliness when she was a child."

"Golly, yes," Freddie piped up. "First her daddy was lost, and then she couldn't live with her mother."

"Yes, it was too bad. But I don't think money can make a person happy. You have to have people to love, and people who love you," Nan said wisely.

Don suddenly seemed to brighten up. He turned and smiled over his shoulder. "You're absolutely right, Nan Bobbsey. Thanks for reminding me."

"But it's too bad Miss Kincaid couldn't remember anything 'bout the seal or the treasure, isn't it?" said Flossie.

"That's right, we still haven't solved *that* mystery," said Bert.

"Yes, our Lakeport treasure hunt does

seem to be flopping," Don Smith agreed with a nod.

"And the worst of it is, we don't even have any more clues to follow," Nan said thoughtfully.

Flossie turned from looking out the car window. "Why not, Nan?"

"Because Miss Kincaid didn't know anything about the town seal, and neither did Mr. Ashton's butler," her sister replied. "They were our only leads."

When Nan mentioned Mr. Ashton's butler, Tweed, Bert sat very still. He was suddenly struck with the thought that Tweed reminded him of someone. But who? It was puzzling.

Next day, Flossie and Freddie went out into the lovely sunny morning to play. Waggo was snoozing happily after Dinah had given him some of the meat she was going to use in her spaghetti sauce for the family's dinner that evening.

So when Mrs. Alton's little calico cat,

Muffin, came bounding over, the twins played with her. Finally, though, they tired of the game and decided to go to the little public park down the street and play on the teeter-totter.

"Oh, Freddie, look!" Flossie had glanced behind her as they reached the open park gate. She pointed to their little playmate, who was following them, her tail waving high in the air.

Freddie laughed and paused to pet Muffin as she caught up with them. "We'd better watch her so she doesn't get lost," he remarked.

The little cat trotted on ahead. But suddenly she stopped and stared intently at something in the grass. Then she crouched down and began creeping forward very slowly. Freddie and Flossie stayed very still, trying to see what Muffin was stalking.

"Ooh, I see now!" Flossie gasped. "Freddie, it's a little field mouse!"

She darted to save the tiny creature.

Flossie was so tenderhearted, she couldn't bear to see anything hurt, even though she didn't really care for mice.

The mouse scurried down a hole by the tree before Muffin could reach it. But the little cat began sniffing and pawing at the hole.

Freddie noticed that the tree looked different somehow from the other trees all around it in the park. Then, as he glanced upward, he saw that it had leaves like lacy ferns.

"Hey, isn't this tree like that one in front of the town hall?" he exclaimed.

Flossie shaded her eyes and peered up at the branches, where her brother was pointing. "Golly, yes, you're right, Freddie! This is another dingo tree!"

"Not a *dingo* tree," said Freddie. "Wasn't it a ginkum tree, or something like that?"

"Well, whatever it was, this is the same kind," declared Flossie. "Maybe

Mr. Ashton gave this one to Lakeport, too."

And, sure enough, on the other side of the tree trunk was a stone with a bronze tablet on it, telling that the tree had been donated by Henry Ashton!

Muffin was still digging away, trying to get at the mouse. The twins watched for a while.

Finally Freddie said, "Come on, Flossie. She won't hurt the mouse." He was tired of just standing and watching. He wanted to ride the teeter-totter.

But Flossie wouldn't leave. "Maybe the mouse has babies. I want to be sure Muffin doesn't hurt them, Freddie. Let's wait. I bet she'll get tired of digging soon."

After a few moments, Muffin suddenly began scratching away at a new spot, a little to one side of where she had been digging before. Then Freddie noticed something shiny and glassy-looking

under the pawed-up turf.

He bent down for a closer look. Getting a stick, he used it to dig down deeper.

"Flossie, look!" he exclaimed. "There's a bottle down there." He had to use both hands to pull it up out of the hole.

"There's something in it, Freddie," said his sister.

The bottle was too dirty to see very well through the glass. Freddie unscrewed the cap. Then he reached inside with his fingers and pulled out a folded piece of paper.

Flossie's eyes grew big as he unfolded it. "Freddie," she cried, "it's some kind of map!"

· 9 ·

The Twirly Clue

There was a sort of jagged or zigzag line
on the paper drawn in red pencil. It led
from an X mark to a little flag. It was
enclosed inside an oblong border or outline, like a picture frame.

There were other markings, too. These
were in ordinary black pencil. They
were mostly straight or crisscross lines,
but there was also a long curving line at
one side of the picture.

Freddie thought his sister was right—
the markings did make the picture look
like a map. "Maybe it's a *treasure* map!"

he cried, hopping up and down with excitement.

"What does this mean?" said Flossie in a puzzled voice. She pointed to a tiny drawing of a telephone underneath the oblong outline, with the letters COV alongside it.

Freddie shrugged. "Search me. Maybe Bert or Nan will know. Let's go ask them!"

"Oh yes, let's!" Flossie gave Freddie back the map and picked Muffin up in her arms, so the little calico cat would not get lost. Then she scampered out of the park with her brother.

On the way home, as they crossed the street, Freddie glanced both ways to make sure no cars were coming. Over his shoulder, he saw a man walking along the street. It looked as if he, too, were walking away from the park, and might even be following the twins.

Freddie told himself that was a silly idea. Why should the man be following them? But even so, the thought made him feel a little bit nervous. "Come on! Let's hurry, Flossie!" he urged.

Nan saw the excited looks on the little twins' faces as they came into the house. "What's the matter?" she asked. "Is anything wrong?"

"Freddie found a treasure map!" cried Flossie.

"And I think a man followed us home from the park!" Freddie added. "Maybe he wanted to take the map away from us!"

Bert pulled the curtain aside and peered out the living room window. "I don't see anybody," he reported. "Sure you weren't imagining things, Freddie?"

"We-e-ell . . . it *looked* like he might be following us. But maybe he wasn't." Freddie was relieved that the stranger was no longer in sight.

"Anyhow, what's all this about a treasure map?" Bert went on keenly.

The little twins told how Freddie had found a bottle buried at the foot of the ginkgo tree. Then they showed Nan and Bert the queer drawing that was inside the bottle.

"Gee, it does look like a map!" said Bert.

"But what's it a map *of*?" questioned Flossie. "The park?"

"Well, let's see," her big brother mused. "One end of this red line— maybe the end with the X mark—could be the place where the bottle was buried under the tree."

"But what about the other end?" said Freddie. "There's no flag in the park."

"No, but some of these straight lines and crisscross lines may be streets. If they are, then the flag could be some-place else, quite a way from the park."

"What about that little telephone down there below the map?" said Flossie. "And those three letters, COV, what do they stand for?"

Nan had been studying the drawing with a thoughtful frown. Suddenly she exclaimed, *"Cover!"*

"Cover to what?" asked Bert, shooting his sister a startled glance.

"To the telephone book! The one Mom's garden club sells every year!" Nan hurried out to the front hall and came back carrying the telephone directory.

It had a white plastic cover fitted over its own stiff paper cover. Each time the telephone company put out a new book, the garden club would sell new covers to protect the books from wear and tear. The money earned in this way went to buy flowers and shrubs for parks and other public places. The covers were popular, and most people bought them.

Each year the plastic covers were decorated with a different kind of flower. This year they were decorated with violets. And the front of the cover always bore a simple map of Lakeport.

"Don't you see?" said Nan, holding

the paper with the drawing on it up to the telephone book. "This oblong outline is exactly the same size as the map on the cover."

"Hey, you're right!" said Bert. The paper was thin enough so that they could see through it when he held the drawing over the map on the cover of the telephone directory. "These straight lines *are* streets. There's Main Street, for instance. And this curved line on one side of the drawing fits the shore line of Lakeport harbor!"

"Where does the flag on the picture fit?" Flossie asked breathlessly. Her blue eyes were wide and eager.

"Wait a second," said Bert. First he found a pencil. Then he held the drawing exactly in place over the map on the telephone book cover, and pressed down the pencil point at the end of the red line with the flag.

When he lifted the drawing off, they could see where the pencil point had been pressed.

"It's the town hall!" Nan cried excitedly.

Freddie clapped his hands. "Sure, that has a flag on it! I remember seeing it when Flossie found Mr. Ashton's picture on that stone!"

"Let's go there right now!" said Bert.

The Bobbseys' house was a dozen blocks away from Lakeport's downtown section. Bert would have liked to ride his bike to get to the town hall faster, but the little twins could not ride their tricycles that far, so all four walked. Bert took turns carrying Flossie and Freddie piggyback when they got tired.

"Gee whiz," said Flossie as they came in sight of the town hall, "do you think that map really shows where to find the Lakeport treasure?"

"Why not?" said Bert. "If Mr. Ashton donated that tree in the park, that would sure be a natural place for him to hide a treasure map."

"But where will we look for the treasure in the town hall?" asked Freddie.

"I don't think it's *inside* the town hall," declared Nan. "I think we'll find it outside."

"How come?"

"Don't you remember what Don Smith told us?" his big sister replied with a twinkle. "I mean how Mr. Ashton got angry when his design for the town seal was turned down by the town council. He said if the public or news reporters ever got to the *root* of the matter, they would see how foolish the town councilors were."

"B-but what does that mean?" Freddie puzzled.

"Oh, I get it!" Bert burst out laughing. "To find the treasure, we have to get to the roots—meaning we have to dig down under this ginkgo tree in front of the town hall!"

"Exactly," said Nan, joining in her brother's laughter.

"Oh, boy! Let's start digging!" cried Freddie.

"But we don't have our beach shovels," said Flossie.

"Never mind," said Bert. "I have my jackknife. I'll sharpen some sticks and we'll dig with those."

Soon all four twins were busily probing the ground around the ginkgo tree. Luckily the grass did not grow right up to the tree trunk, so they were able to poke their sticks into bare earth.

"Try to be neat," Nan advised her brothers and sister. "Remember, we'll have to put all this dirt back in place."

"Indeed you will!" boomed an angry voice. "And you'd better start doing it right now!"

The Bobbseys looked up in surprise and saw a man looming over them. It was Mr. Ashton's former butler, Tweed!

"Don't worry, Mr. Tweed, we'll make sure everything looks as nice as before, when we're done," Bert assured him. "But something important may be buried here. We're trying to find it."

"Never mind making excuses! You brats have no right to ruin public property! Stop digging this minute!" As he spoke, Tweed grabbed Bert roughly by the arm and yanked him to his feet.

"And *you* have no right to push me around, so let go!" Bert retorted stoutly.

There might have been a nasty scuffle. But at that moment Don Smith came out of the town hall. He saw at once what was going on and strode over to stop it.

"Better take your hands off that boy, Mr. Tweed," he warned sharply, "or you're going to find yourself in big trouble!"

Tweed started to growl angrily at the reporter. Then he noticed a policeman coming along the street, so he lowered his voice. "I was just trying to stop these young hooligans from messing up the town hall lawn," he grumbled.

"We weren't hurting the lawn," said Flossie.

Meanwhile, both Freddie and Bert were staring intently at the former butler.

"Hey!" Freddie blurted, pointing his

finger at Tweed. "You're the man who followed me and Flossie from the park! I knew I'd just seen you somewhere today!"

"Today isn't the only time he's been around our place," Bert chimed in. He had just realized why the butler had seemed familiar when they visited him at his apartment in Shoreview. "You're the guy who came to our house and tried to get Flossie's music box. Only then you wore a fake mustache and pretended your name was Crane!"

Tweed had turned first red in the face and then pale while Bert was talking. The policeman was coming closer all the time. Without waiting for him to reach the scene, the butler suddenly turned and tried to dart away.

But Freddie thrust out one foot and tripped him before he could escape. Tweed went sprawling in the grass!

As he did so, something fell out of his coat pocket. It was a chain with a pocket-

knife on one end and a little flashlight attached to the other end. Something clicked in Flossie's memory. All of a sudden she knew where she had seen that chain before.

"Bert's right!" she cried. "That's what Mr. Crane kept twirling when he came to our house that time!"

Just then the policeman came hurrying up. "What's going on here?" he asked.

When he heard the Bobbseys' whole story, he was ready to arrest Tweed on the spot. But the twins thought it best to wait and let their parents decide whether or not to press charges, since there might be no way to prove Tweed was also the burglar who had tried to break into their house at night.

At that moment, the twins were much more interested in completing their treasure hunt. So now they resumed digging while the policeman and bystanders looked on.

Nan gave a cry of excitement. "I think I've found something!"

Bert whistled and exclaimed as he saw her fingers uncover a gleaming yellow object. "Looks like you've struck gold!"

·10·

Secret Treasure

Everyone crowded closer and watched with bated breath as Nan worked eagerly to clear away the dirt from around her find.

She had stopped using her sharpened stick for fear of scratching the shiny yellow treasure. Now she was digging with her hands and fingers. In a few moments she unearthed the object.

The onlookers gasped and cheered as she held it up in full view. "The boy was right," one exclaimed. "That thing must be solid gold!"

Nan smiled and nodded. "I'll bet it is, too!" Like the other Bobbseys, she had learned on an earlier adventure how heavy gold feels. And this was certainly a hefty little handful!

"No doubt about it," said Don Smith. "Only gold would stay so shiny after being buried in the ground!"

"But what is it?" asked Flossie, her blue eyes bigger than ever. Freddie stared at it, too.

"Can't you guess?" Nan twinkled at them.

The object was about three inches high and in the shape of a cylinder. It had a gold ball on top with a dove perched on it, serving as a handle. It looked like a beautiful golden paper-weight. On the bottom was a flat plastic cap.

Freddie scratched his head and shrugged. "Isn't it that treasure Mr. Ashton told everyone about?"

"Sure." Bert chuckled. "But don't you

remember *why* he was offering Lakeport a treasure?"

Freddie and Flossie looked puzzled. They didn't understand what Bert meant. Neither did most of the people watching—except for Don Smith. He and the older twins had guessed right away what the object was for.

Nan pried off the plastic cap. Now Freddie and Flossie could see a steel disk fitted into the bottom of the cylinder. The disk had a picture and words carved on it.

Suddenly Flossie snapped her fingers and cried, "Now I know! That's the *town seal!*"

"Right!" said Nan with a triumphant smile. "The town seal that Mr. Ashton hired Belinda Wardell to design."

"Imagine! Made out of pure gold!" one spectator remarked to another. "That thing must be worth a small fortune!"

Don Smith turned to Tweed, who was

eyeing the Lakeport treasure greedily.
"So that's what you were after, eh?"

"I don't know what you're talking
about," the sullen ex-butler mumbled.

"Oh, yes you do! You probably knew
all along what the treasure was that Mr.
Ashton was talking about. But you didn't
know where he'd hidden it. At first you
thought there might be a clue in the
Wardell girl's music box. So you went to
the Bobbseys' house in disguise and
tried to get hold of it. When you couldn't,
you still kept spying on the Bobbsey
twins, hoping they might solve the mystery. Today they did—and you tried to
stop them so you could dig up the treasure first!"

"You're crazy!" growled Tweed.
"You're just making up a pack of lies to
try and get a headline news story." But
his guilty expression showed that Don's
charges were all too true.

Tweed turned and once again tried to
walk away fast. This time it was the

policeman who stopped him by grabbing his arm.

"Hold on, mister!" the officer snapped. "I'm not through with you yet!"

He took down Tweed's name and address and warned him not to leave town until the proper authorities decided if he should be tried for any crime.

Meanwhile, Don Smith and some of the onlookers accompanied the Bobbsey twins into the town hall, so they could present the treasure they had found to the mayor of Lakeport.

The mayor had his secretary type an official letter of thanks to the Bobbseys. After signing the paper, he affixed a blob of red wax and stamped it with the seal, so everyone could see what the design looked like.

Don Smith snapped their pictures and telephoned the story to the *Lakeport News*. A TV crew also arrived to interview the four children.

Later, Don drove the twins home.

Mrs. Bobbsey invited him to dinner to celebrate the solving of the mystery.

That evening, the whole family and their guest were seated around the table when the television news broadcast began. Mr. and Mrs. Bobbsey watched proudly as the youngsters were interviewed and then handed a letter of thanks by the mayor. Dinah and Sam Johnson also watched, sharing the family's enjoyment.

The broadcast was barely over when the telephone rang. Dinah answered.

"It's a lawyer named Mr. Weaver," she reported. "He's calling to inquire about Charlotte Wardell."

"Well, twins, I think you know the most about that subject," Mr. Bobbsey said with a smile.

Bert listened on the phone as the caller explained that his law firm was trying to find Charlotte Wardell, in order to pay her the royalty money due on her father's boat design. "Oh, yes," Bert replied. "We told her about that, Mr. Weaver. She's getting in touch with Mr. Durkee."

"Durkee?" The caller sounded upset. "That fellow's no lawyer! He's a crooked clerk who used to work in our office. We fired him!"

When Bert told the others, Nan immediately tried to phone Charlotte and warn her. But she got a busy signal.

"Never mind calling," Don Smith said anxiously. "I vote we drive there and tell her in person!"

It was almost eight o'clock when they arrived at Charlotte's apartment building in Center City. Don Smith rang her bell in the vestibule and explained over the door phone. "I'm here with the Bobbsey twins, Miss Kincaid. We've something important to tell you. May we come up?"

"Yes, of course." Charlotte buzzed them in.

When the slender young woman opened her door, Don and the twins could see that she had a visitor. Flossie gasped, "It's Mr. Durkee!"

He was standing by a table with a paper and pen on it. Don strode toward him angrily while the twins told Charlotte about Mr. Weaver's call.

"Oh, my goodness." She turned shocked eyes on Durkee. "What really is on that paper you wanted me to sign, Mr. Durkee?"

Don picked up the paper to read it aloud. The fake lawyer gave him a hard shove and tried to snatch it away.

"You cheating crook!" Don blurted angrily and punched Durkee on the jaw. As he toppled to the floor, Don went on in disgust, "Trying to get her to sign all her royalties over to you!"

"Thank goodness you didn't sign anything!" Nan exclaimed to the pretty young teacher.

"My dears, you arrived just in time!" Charlotte replied happily. Then she hugged and kissed each of the twins in turn.

"Don't I rate one, too?" Don Smith asked.

Blushing, Charlotte kissed him shyly on the cheek, and his arm slid around her waist.

The Bobbsey twins exchanged satisfied nods. They wondered if their next adventure, *The Ghost in the Computer*, would have the same happy ending.

"I think she'll be his fi-nancee soon!" Flossie whispered.

"Oh, Flossie!" Nan giggled. "You mean *fiancée*."